Date Due			
8			
2			
3			

DeJong, David Cornel
Looking For Alexander

Looking
for
Alexander

Looking
for
Alexander

by
David Cornel DeJong

Illustrated by
Harvey Weiss

An Atlantic Monthly Press Book
Little, Brown and Company · Boston · Toronto

LIBRARY OF CONGRESS CATALOG CARD NO. 63-7681

Second Printing

ATLANTIC—LITTLE, BROWN BOOKS
ARE PUBLISHED BY
LITTLE, BROWN AND COMPANY
IN ASSOCIATION WITH
THE ATLANTIC MONTHLY PRESS

*Published simultaneously in Canada
by Little, Brown & Company (Canada) Limited*

PRINTED IN THE UNITED STATES OF AMERICA

This book is emphatically dedicated to my brother Raymond's grandchildren, who are, as of June 1962:

Gary, Linda, Suzann and Teddy Lynema,
Keith, Mark and Kathy DeYoung,
Bruce, Craig, Raette and Daniel Kaiserlian.

CHAPTER ONE

IT WAS VERY EARLY in the morning. The sun had just begun to rise and no one could see it but Alexander the Great, who was sitting on the top of the tallest flagpole in town.

Alexander had been on the flagpole all night long. The pole was so thin and slippery that he couldn't get down, and it kept swaying in the wind. Alexander had been up there since eight o'clock last evening, when a pack of dogs had chased him across the field, into the little park, and then up the flagpole. With the dogs yapping and snarling below him, Alexander had kept climbing until he reached the top of the pole and the top of the golden ball at the very tip of the tall flagpole.

After the dogs had left, Alexander had tried to climb down. It was impossible. He had cried and meowed but no one had heard him, perhaps because the little park was so far from the houses, or because the wind had made the leaves rustle so loud. By midnight Alexander had meowed so long and so loud that he was hoarse.

Far off he could see the house where he lived with young David. Before it got dark he had even seen David walk around the house looking for him and calling him. He had seen David's grandmother ride off on her bicycle looking for him along the street. He had heard David's father and mother call his name from the front door of the house.

Then dusk had come, and then night. Lights went on in the house. He had tried to meow again, but his voice wouldn't come out. And the night became darker and the wind stronger. Even so, very late at night, he had heard David's voice, and David had called, "Alexander, Alexander, where are you?" He could not see David, even though like all cats he could see in the dark.

But David's room was on the other side of the house, so David must have called from his window.

Alexander was very cold and very lonely. Now, however, the sun was up, and pretty soon someone was sure to see him.

After a while he could see Jack and Joe open up their Service Station and Greasing Palace. Jack and Joe were young David's friends, and Alexander knew them very well.

Far away, on the other side of town, near the railroad station, he saw Mrs. Twill come out of her house to work in her garden. Mrs. Twill was a baby sitter, and Alexander knew her well, too. Sometimes he had even followed her home.

But those were the only people he saw. Even

Sam hadn't come out yet to sweep the sidewalk in front of his second-hand shop. And Mr. Bim, the tailor, had not yet looked out of his window over the shop to see what kind of weather it was.

Then Alexander saw David's father drive off to work in the city. He saw David's mother and grandmother come out of the house, and he heard them call his name. But they never looked high enough or far enough.

CHAPTER TWO

WHEN David woke up he was surprised that he had been asleep. He had planned to stay awake all night and wait for Alexander.

Once, in the middle of the night, he had called Alexander from his open window. But that had waked up the baby, and Mother had told him to

go back to sleep because Alexander would be sure to be back home when he woke up.

He had not wanted to sleep, but he had. And now he woke up as he heard his father start the car to go to work. He heard Mother and Grandmother talking outdoors.

David jumped out of bed and ran downstairs. He could tell at once from the way Mother and Grandmother looked at him that Alexander had not come back. Then his mother made him sit down and eat his breakfast.

"You have to eat your breakfast, David. You need your strength to look for Alexander. And then you and Grandmother can start looking."

"Yes, Mother," David said, but he could not eat.

12

"We'll go all over town, and all around town,"
Grandmother said.

"Yes, Grandmother," David said and tried to
swallow.

13

"We'll look high and low, and far and wide, and left and right, and east and west and north and south," Grandmother said.

David nodded and blinked back his tears.

"I'll go on my bicycle," Grandmother said, "so that I can look far and wide and fast. And David, you can go on foot and start close to the house. You know where all of Alexander's favorite places are much better than I do. After all, I just come here once in a while for a few days. Besides, David, he will come when you call him."

David looked down at his breakfast plate.

"I think you two had better get started at once," Mother scolded. "Neither you nor your grandmother has eaten more than two spoonfuls."

Even before she was through speaking, David had jumped up. He ran upstairs to put on his clothes. He dressed in less than two minutes and he knew that Mother was too upset to stop him to see if he was dressed properly.

Grandmother was already seated on her bicycle, and when he came outside she shouted, "I'm off, David. I'll go down every street and every alley and every road I can find."

"Yes, Grandmother, and I'll look in every hole and corner close to the house and in the field," David said, but Grandmother was already pedaling away.

"Alexander, Alexander, come Alexander," David started shouting.

CHAPTER THREE

FIRST David looked in the garage. Then he walked all around the garage. He looked all through the orchard and beneath the grapevine, all the time calling Alexander's name. Then he crossed the field in back of the house, because the field was really Alexander's field, where he

spent hours trying to catch field mice. Usually he stayed close to the large white stone in the middle of the field.

This time Alexander wasn't on the white stone or near it. Even from the top of the stone David could not see anything. He crossed the field, and crossed it again; he crisscrossed it and circled it, all the time calling: "Alexander, Alexander, where are you?" He peered into every rabbit hole, and he looked beneath every bush in the field, and up every tree. He found nothing.

Three times he had come past Jack and Joe's Service Station and Greasing Palace on the far side of the field. Each time both Jack and Joe were very busy, and the truth was David felt so sad he didn't even feel like talking to Jack and Joe.

But the fourth time he had to tell them that Alexander was lost.

"Oh no! Not Alexander the Great," Joe said.

"Not your Alexander! That's impossible," Jack shouted.

David nodded. "He was gone all night, Jack and Joe."

"Oh, but cats always go away and they always come back. I once had a cat that was gone three weeks," Joe said.

"And I heard of a cat that was gone three years and then came back as if nothing had happened," Jack said.

This time David didn't say anything. He simply couldn't wait three years for Alexander. He couldn't even think of waiting that long.

Then Jack had to hurry off and put gasoline in a car, and Joe said: "Do you know what the trouble is, Davie? You haven't got your wonderful birthday umbrella. If you carried your umbrella, and Alexander saw it and heard all its bells tinkling, he'd come running."

It was true, both David and Grandmother had

worried so much about the lost cat that they hadn't even remembered the big yellow umbrella, with its four windows, purple fringes, blinker top, flamingo handle and all its silver bells. And Alexander loved that umbrella.

Jack and Joe's Garage

"I am going to run home and get that umbrella," David cried, suddenly all excited.

"And if you don't find Alexander by six o'clock tonight," Joe shouted, "come and tell us. We'll help you look for him. Today we are so busy, we haven't a minute to spare."

But David wasn't even listening. Not really listening, because he knew he couldn't wait till six o'clock. He'd have to find Alexander long before that. Long, long before that, or else...

CHAPTER FOUR

BACK home, David raised his large umbrella at once. He looked out through all its four windows to see how much he could see. He could look in all directions, that was true, though he couldn't look very high. On the other hand, Grandmother on her bicycle would be looking far and wide and high.

And he knew that Alexander would be able to see the large yellow umbrella from a long way off. He'd certainly hear all the bells on it, if he was anywhere near.

Again David crossed and crisscrossed the field. He climbed on top of the white stone and twirled the umbrella, so that all the bells jingled and jangled clearly. He peered through all the four windows. He saw nothing. Nothing happened.

Again he circled the field four times. He could see how busy Jack and Joe were. They would wave at him as he came by, but they had no time to talk. Twice, too, he saw Grandmother go pedaling by in the distance, still looking left and right, far and wide.

Then David remembered the little path that

crossed a meadow and circled all around town and ended up at the railroad station. Alexander knew about the path. He often wandered that way to go to the creek, to watch the fishes in the creek and the butterflies fluttering over.

David hurried down the little crooked path. He saw birds and butterflies and in the creek he saw minnows, but he did not see Alexander. When he came to the railroad fence, he was going to turn back, but then he saw Mrs. Twill's house across from the station. Mrs. Twill always knew about everything, everything that was lost and found even. And Mrs. Twill knew Alexander very well.

Mrs. Twill was in her garden pruning rose-bushes, and when she heard the bells of David's umbrella, she turned and waved and called, "Now

26

David, what brings you here so early in the day?"

"Alexander is lost, Mrs. Twill. He was gone all night."

"Impossible," Mrs. Twill said. "Alexander is too nice a cat to be lost."

"But he is, Mrs. Twill."

"Ah, we must think, David," Mrs. Twill cried, and she pulled hairpins out of her hair and put them back again in order to think better. "Have you looked right and left, David?"

"Yes, and far and wide, Mrs. Twill. And east and west and north and south. And Grandmother is on her bicycle looking."

"Well, your grandmother shouldn't be on a bicycle. Grandmothers just shouldn't. It might scare Alexander away from house and home. Did you ever think of that, David?"

"No, Mrs. Twill," David said.

"Well, maybe I'm wrong. Except I think I know where your Alexander is," Mrs. Twill said seriously.

"Where, Mrs. Twill?"

"Oh I am sure. That is I have a feeling that he's gone back to Farmer Brown's farm. That's where Alexander was born, remember? He's gone back to call on his mother and sisters and brothers."

David shook his head. Mrs. Twill seemed to think of cats as if they were human beings. "But that was three years ago, Mrs. Twill."

"That doesn't matter. He was lonesome for his mother."

"And Farmer Brown's farm is ten miles away," David cried.

"A mere trifle for a cat. Besides, I'm going there next month and I'll have a look around then. I'm terribly busy now. I have a cake to bake, bushes to prune, everything. Ah, but I see that the purple fringe on your umbrella is getting loose. Let me run in the house and get some purple thread and sew it on again. Now you just wait."

But David could not wait to have the fringe sewed. He shouted, "Goodbye, Mrs. Twill," and hurried away. But she didn't even hear, she was so set on getting the purple thread.

As he kept running with all the bells of his

umbrella tinkling, David saw through its front window that Grandmother was waiting for him down the street. She had gotten off her bicycle and she was talking to Mr. Bim, the tailor, and to Sam, who had the second-hand shop.

CHAPTER FIVE

GRANDMOTHER must have told Sam and Mr. Bim all about Alexander, because Sam said at once, "Oh Davie, I have looked all through my shop for Alexander. I looked in every nook and crook, in every cranny and corner. Alas, I found nothing."

Sam looked as if he had done exactly that. He was covered with dust and he had cobwebs all through his hair.

Mr. Bim said, "And I looked all through my tailor shop, in every bolt of cloth. And I found nothing, Davie."

David was so close to crying that he kept his
umbrella over him, and Sam and Mr. Bim talked
to him through the little windows of the umbrella.

"And my motto is," Sam said, squinting hard
at David, "you must keep looking far and wide

and high and dry . . . oh, I mean low; and east, west, north and south, David."

"And I would come right with you and help you, Davie," Sam said, "but I have a big load of old baby buggies, radios and old sleds coming in and I have to stay right here."

"And I have to measure a tall man for a new suit because he is getting married next week, Davie," Mr. Bim said.

At last David could say, "Yes, Sam. Yes, Mr. Bim. And thank you," but his voice started choking.

Grandmother must have heard that he was close to crying, because suddenly she ducked right under the umbrella with him and held his hand, and she said to Sam at the one window and to Mr. Bim at the other, "Thank you very much, gentlemen. But now we must go and find Alexander."

Then he and Grandmother hurried away beneath the umbrella, and to cheer up David, she sang, "Oh, we'll look high and low, we'll look far and wide, we'll look east and west, and we'll look north and south, and we'll find Alexander "

She was so busy trying to cheer him up that they had reached the end of the street before she remembered that she had left her bicycle in front of Mr. Bim's tailor shop. She had to run back and get it.

CHAPTER SIX

WHILE he waited for Grandmother to get her bicycle, David sat down on the curb. He felt so miserable, he sat very low, so that the great umbrella covered him completely. He felt so sad he didn't even look through the windows of the umbrella.

Then, to cheer himself up a bit, he started sing-ing Grandmother's little ditty.

Oh, we'll look high and low,
We'll look far and wide,
We'll look east and west,
We'll look north and south,
And we'll find Alexander.

But they had looked everywhere, he and Grandmother. And even Sam and Mr. Bim. Even in dark corners and holes. Except . . .

David had just started singing again, "Oh, we'll look high . . ." when he stopped. But they hadn't looked high. Not really. On the other hand, Alexander wouldn't be flying in the sky. Of course, he might be on a roof or in a tree, but in that case he'd come down. Cats always did.

Just then Grandmother came back with her
bicycle and David jumped up shouting, "Grandmother, we haven't looked high."

"Well, perhaps not very high," Grandmother said.

"Not as high as the sky," David cried.

"But what would he be doing in the sky, David? Unless . . ." and Grandmother peered up into the sky.

"Unless?" David said.

"Unless it is something very high. And he can't come down."

Something high and thin, and maybe slippery, David thought. A flagpole? And he knew of one very tall flagpole, the tallest one in town, in the little park only two blocks from home. And he had never looked that far or that high, and Grandmother must have cycled right beneath it without looking up. Or perhaps she hadn't been able to see the flagpole above the trees when she bicycled along the road.

"The flagpole. The flagpole," David shouted. And he started running beneath his umbrella, with all the bells jangling and jingling, because he didn't want to take time to close the umbrella.

Grandmother was so surprised she could only stare after him. She didn't know anything about any flagpole. She hadn't seen a flagpole. But there was David racing across a field full of brambles and bushes and weeds.

Grandmother hopped on her bicycle and tried to follow him. But she couldn't cross that field, so she kept going down the road, and each time she saw someone she shouted, "Where is the flagpole, please?" But she couldn't stop to get their

answer, because she had to keep her eye on David
and she had to keep up with him, and the road

42

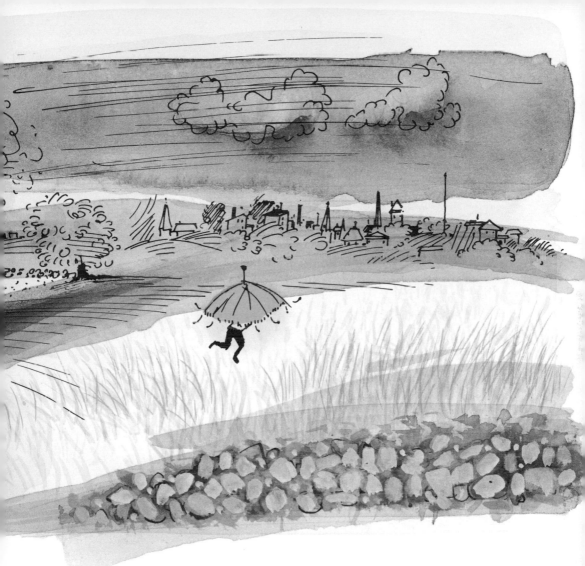

seemed much farther around than the field. And
David was running very fast.

CHAPTER SEVEN

DAVID kept running across the field. He ran straight for the little park in which the flagpole stood, even though he could not see the flagpole above the trees because the windows in his umbrella were not high enough.

That was the trouble—the windows were not

high or wide enough. Suddenly David pushed
the umbrella up by its fancy flamingo handle
and let it fly over his head, with all its bells tinkling madly. He had no time for the umbrella

now. He didn't even have time to see it sail away and come tumbling down, to sit like a great big yellow flower in the middle of the field.

Because now, without the umbrella, David could see the flagpole above the trees. He looked for the golden ball on top of the pole, but the golden ball this time was something much larger, and it wasn't golden, but black and white, and it had a tail. It was a cat. It was Alexander the Great! And Alexander was watching him as he came racing across the field.

Just when David had to cross the road to the little park, there came Grandmother racing on her bicycle. David shouted, "There, there, on top of the flagpole."

Grandmother hopped off her bicycle. But she

could not see the flagpole because of all the trees around it.

When David reached her he kept pointing up and shouting, even though he couldn't see the pole himself now. But he kept running on into the little park, to the foot of the flagpole, and Grandmother came running after him.

And then, as they looked up—it seemed like miles up—there on the very top of the thin flag-pole sat poor Alexander, on the small gold ball.

"Oh, we can never get him down, David," Grandmother cried. "He can never get down that thin pole himself."

David didn't know what to say. He just stared up, and poor Alexander stared down and opened his mouth to cry but didn't make any sound.

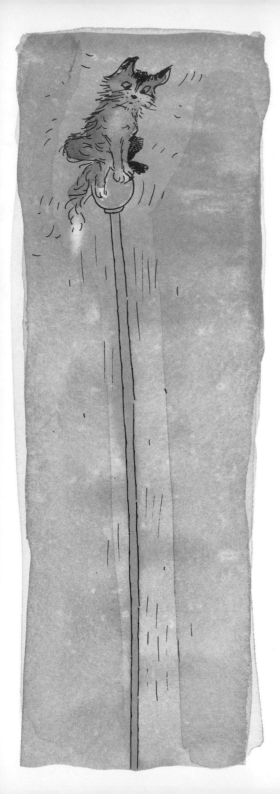

"We have to think, David," Grandmother cried.

David thought about Jack and Joe. They could climb, but this pole was altogether too thin and shaky. And Sam wouldn't do, nor Mr. Bim, and surely not Mrs. Twill.

He could hear poor Alexander meow. It was a very hoarse and low sound. "Oh, he must have been crying all night,"

David said, and he tried to think harder.

Now that they were there Alexander tried to climb down, but each time he shifted a paw the whole pole shook so hard that he had to clutch the gold ball for dear life.

Then David had an idea. "The flag. The flag, Grandmother," he shouted. "If we pull the flag up, maybe Alexander could come down on the flag."

But there was no flag. Today wasn't a holiday. And neither David nor Grandmother knew where the flag was kept. There were only the ropes dangling down from the top of the pole.

Then David had another idea. "My umbrella," he cried. "My birthday umbrella."

"Where is it? Did you lose it, David? Anyway,

this is no time for your umbrella," Grandmother said.

"Oh yes it is. We'll raise the umbrella like a flag. We'll tie it on the ropes and raise it up to Alexander. And then Alexander can come down on the umbrella, Grandmother."

"Wonderful!" Grandmother cried. "But where is your umbrella?"

David was no longer there. She saw him run out of the little park and across the road and into the field. There in the middle of the field Grandmother saw the umbrella like a large yellow flower, and David went running straight for it.

Then David was back with the umbrella, with all its bells tinkling, and Alexander was staring down from the top of the flagpole.

50

And then once more they failed. They could not tie the open umbrella to the flag ropes, no matter how they tried. The umbrella was altogether too wide and too clumsy to handle. But when the umbrella was closed, it wouldn't be of much help either.

"Except, Grandmother," David said. "Except, if we open it up just a little. Just open enough so that we can pull it up the pole, and Alexander can jump inside."

"Oh, something like a big ice cream cone," Grandmother cried.

That was it. Like a large ice cream cone. They closed the umbrella, and they tried to open it a little, but it would not stay that way. It went either wide open, or it closed up tight. And all the

time poor Alexander kept crying more hoarsely.

Then David had still another idea. "Shoes, my shoes," he cried.

Grandmother knew at once what he meant. When David pulled off his shoes, she took hers off, too, and then they wedged the shoes like cross-pieces just above the spokes inside the umbrella. It made the umbrella stay open just enough, and it did look like a large cone, and Alexander would be able to get inside it.

Once more they tied the partly opened umbrella to the flag ropes. This time it worked. When David and Grandmother pulled on the other rope, the umbrella went straight up the pole, with the flamingo handle up top and the red blinker at the bottom and with the little bells tinkling merrily.

Up above it, Alexander looked down. His eyes for a moment went very round and frightened. Then he saw that it was the birthday umbrella coming right up the pole toward him.

CHAPTER EIGHT

THE UMBRELLA reached the top of the flagpole. In fact, its long flamingo handle reached
so high that it almost pushed Alexander off the
golden ball.

But Alexander was no longer frightened. He
seemed to know what he had to do. When the

54

flamingo handle pushed him, he started twisting and turning. He slid, and he almost tumbled.
Then he grabbed hold of the curved neck of the
flamingo head, and twisting some more, and
meowing louder, he slid down it like a fireman,
right into the cup of the half-open umbrella.

From down below David and Grandmother

could see him land and make a bulge, where the shoes were wedged. But Alexander had come tumbling so hard that now the umbrella started coming down all by itself, and David had to grab hold of the rope and hold it tight to keep it from tumbling down too fast.

Then it was there, at the bottom of the flag-pole. Both he and Grandmother reached for the umbrella and looked into it. There was Alexander, curled up on the shoes, looking round-eyed and excited.

David didn't know whether he should laugh or cry. He felt like doing both at once. It was all so wonderful. "Can't we carry Alexander home just like this, Grandmother?" he asked. "Like this, in the umbrella. He must be very tired."

"Of course, of course," Grandmother said. "We don't need our shoes. Alexander needs them more than we do."

They took the flag ropes off the umbrella, and tied them to the pole again. Then very carefully they carried the umbrella between them with Alexander inside and all the little bells tinkling over Alexander's head.

Because of the tinkling, and because they were
so happy and excited, they hadn't heard the
shouting. Then they heard it, and there, running
across the field, came Jack and Joe, and behind

them Sam, and still farther behind was Mr. Bim and far behind Mr. Bim came Mrs. Twill. They were all waving and shouting, all at once, "We saw the yellow umbrella go up like a flag. And then we saw Alexander up top. And then we just came running...."

David and Grandmother had to wait for them. They all came and looked down at Alexander inside the umbrella. Mrs. Twill was the last to reach them, and she still carried a needle and purple thread.

And then they all marched home. Mr. Bim and Sam pushed Grandmother's bicycle between them. Mrs. Twill kept making sewing motions with her needle, even though she was a yard behind the umbrella and even though Jack and Joe were walking between her and the umbrella, trying to get another look at Alexander inside. And everybody was laughing and chattering, and nobody seemed to notice that David and Grandmother wore no shoes at all.